Blue Dot Kids Press

www.BlueDotKidsPress.com

Original North American edition published in 2020 by Blue Dot Kids Press, PO Box 2344,
San Francisco, CA 94126. Blue Dot Kids Press is a trademark of Blue Dot Publications LLC.

BLUE D●T KIDS PRESS

Cataloging in Publication Data is available from the United States Library of Congress.

ISBN: 9781733121286

FSC
www.fsc.org
MIX
Paper from
responsible sources
FSC™ C136333

The illustrations in the book are hand-painted using
watercolor paint, gouache, graphite and ink pencil, and chinagraph pencil.

Printed in China with soy inks.

First Printing

Welcome Home, Whales

Written and Illustrated by

Christina Booth

BLUE DOT KIDS PRESS

When I first heard her call, it came from the bay,
echoing off the mountain like a whisper
while the moon danced on the waves.

Mom hadn't heard anything.
Dad couldn't hear it either.

"Perhaps you were dreaming,"
said Grandma.

Yet each morning I hear her call.

Each day she comes closer,
telling me something new.

Sometimes she is full of joy.

Sometimes she is sad.
It tugs at my heart as I listen.

Her stories grow louder,
carried beneath the breath of the wind.
I snuggle under the blankets
until she wakes me from my dreams.

Now I know.

I know why she is calling me.

I bundle up against the cold
and run to the edge of the bay.
I wait for her by the night-sky water
and listen to the waves push in
and out against the shore.

I hear her story.
She tells me of her fears and sorrows.
Her story turns inside my head
and twists around my heart,
and I don't want to listen anymore.
I want to run away, but I stay,
looking for her in the cold winter dawn.

As dark shifts to gray, I see her.
She sees me and comes in closer to the shore.

"We wanted to come home,
but we did not feel safe," she says.
"Why did they hurt us?
Why did they send us away?"

I hang my head.
It wasn't me, but I know what she means.

I do not know what to say.
I only have one word to tell her.

"Sorry," I whisper.

My heart aches
as she turns and swims away,
slapping her flukes
like a clap of thunder on the waves.

She is gone.

As the sun lifts into the sky,
I see her again, out in the bay.
People gather on the shore
to watch her in the winter dawn.

I hear her calling again,
softly and gently, but not to me.

A small tail lifts out of the waves.
A steamy spout breaches
the water.

Her baby lifts its head
to greet us.

Now I hear two voices calling
with a story of new beginnings,
of hope and forgiveness.

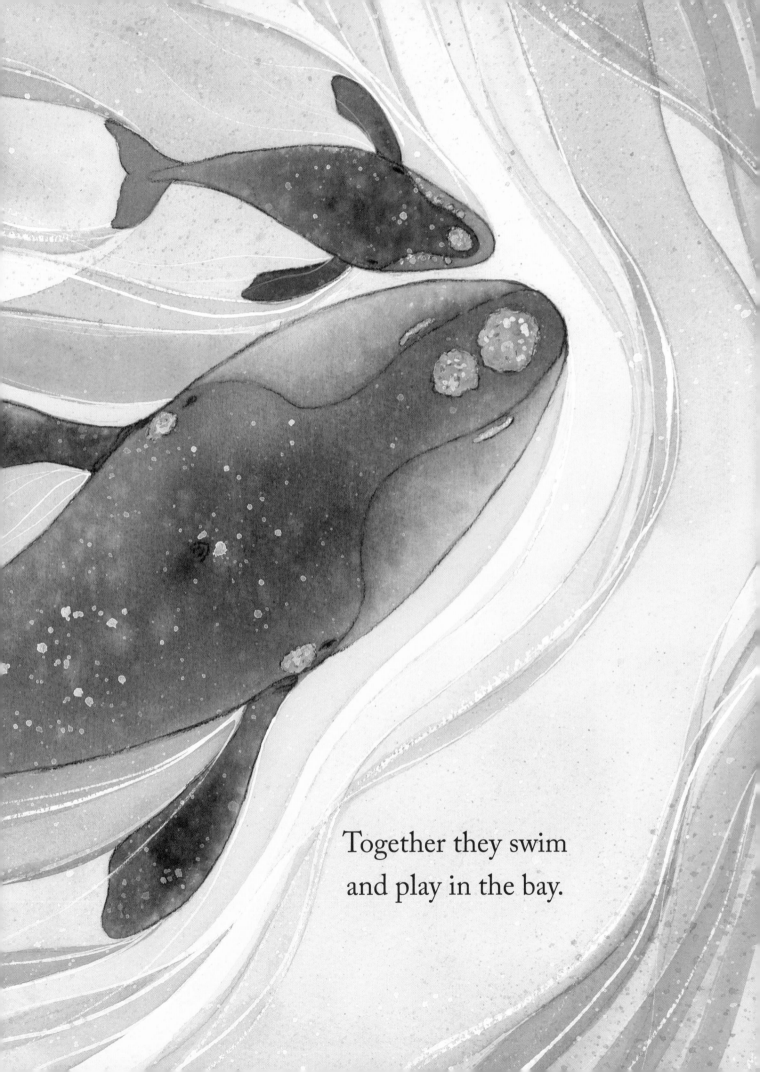

Together they swim
and play in the bay.

"Welcome home," I say.

"Welcome home,"
echoes the mountain.

krill, actual size

There are three species of right whales. North Atlantic right whales live in the North Atlantic Ocean, mostly along the east coast of North America. They spend summers feeding off the northeastern coasts of Canada and the United States. In winter, they head south toward Georgia and Florida to give birth (called calving). North Pacific right whales live in the Bering Sea, which is between Alaska and Russia.

Right whales are baleen whales. Baleen are long strands of hairlike fibers inside the whale's mouth that filter seawater for krill, the tiny shrimplike creatures that right whales eat. They use their tongues to collect the krill and flip them back into their throats.

Callosities

Right whales got their name because they were the favorite of whalers, who hunted them hundreds of years ago. They were hunted for their blubber, baleen, tongues, and bones, which people used to make oil for lamps and machines, soap, fabrics, umbrellas, and more.

The large white patches on right whales are called callosities. They are made of calcium and microscopic creatures. A whale's callosity patterns are as unique as human fingerprints.

Hunting right whales was banned worldwide in 1935, when they were on the verge of going extinct. Today they are also protected under the Endangered Species Act and the Marine Mammal Protection Act in the United States.

Pots for extracting whale oil

Even with these protections, the North Atlantic and North Pacific right whales are two of the most endangered species in the world. As of 2020, there are only about four hundred North Atlantic right whales and just over one hundred North Pacific right whales alive. Conservation efforts have been more successful with Southern right whales, whose population has slowly increased to around ten thousand whales.

The third species of right whale is the Southern right whale. They live in the oceans of the Southern Hemisphere, the half of Earth that is south of the equator. They spend summers feeding in the waters around Antarctica and winters calving along the coasts of New Zealand, Australia, southern Africa, and South America.

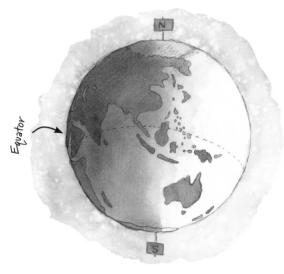

You can identify a right whale by its "V"-shaped spray.

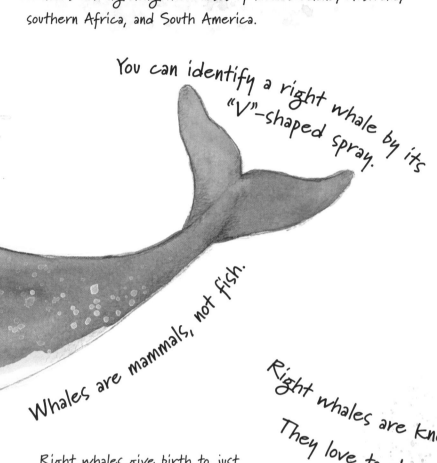

Whales are mammals, not fish.

All right whales are migratory, moving seasonally to feed or give birth. The warm waters at the equator form a barrier that keeps the northern and southern species separate from one another.

Right whales are known for their acrobatics. They love to play.

Right whales give birth to just one calf every three to five years, versus other species of whales that may give birth every one to three years. This low birth rate makes it hard for them to increase their population size.

Although right whales can no longer be hunted, two common threats remain: being struck by ships and getting tangled in fishing gear. As we work to fix these human-caused problems and whales learn to trust us again, we hope to see more of them returning to our waters.

Do you live near an ocean?

What types of whales swim in the ocean where you live?

If you don't live near an ocean, are you planning a trip to visit an ocean this year?

What types of whales live there?

We can welcome our whale neighbors home and help keep them safe.

You can help whales wherever you live. You have a voice to do so.
Here are four actions that you can do today:

- Read and learn about the oceans and their inhabitants. Learn about what impact we humans have on whale homes.

- Write to your elected officials, like a senator or the president, about why whales are important to you and that you want our government to take steps to protect them.

- If you live in a state or territory that has beaches along the Atlantic or Pacific, write to your governor, asking them to help protect the whales that call your area's waters home.

- Help keep plastics out of waterways. All our creeks, streams, and rivers eventually empty into the ocean. Protect ocean creatures by collecting and disposing of any plastic trash you see in bodies of water near your home or wherever you travel.

To find out more about important whale conservation efforts nationwide—including the protection of right whales, orca whales, and beluga whales—visit the nonprofit wildlife conservation organization Defenders of Wildlife online at defenders.org.

One percent of proceeds from sales of this book will be donated to Defenders of Wildlife.